She opened the refrigerator and saw Vegan butter spread, Fage greek yogurt, extra firm tofu, and a variety of Kombucha drinks and flavored kefir. So Barry was a health food hippie. He'd gone for the salad and breadsticks at the restaurant. Were they gluten free? She didn't know. Did the butter make a difference? All organic or something? Or was he not that strict about it when he was out?

She brought the drink to him.

"Thanks," he said. "Did you get something for yourself, too?"

"I didn't see anything I liked. Are you a vegan?"

His eyes widened for a moment. "I haven't shown you my penis yet, how could you know that?"

Also by Ann L. Probe

How to Get Abducted by UFO Aliens: A Short and Stubby Guide to Having Sex with Extraterrestrials

The Alien Sex Chronicles

1. Boffing Bigfoot
2. Fifty Slaves of Grays
3. Tall White and Hung
4. Mounting the Mothman
5. Ravaged by the Reptilian
6. The Nordic Nymphos
7. Sleeping with the Alien
8. The Sexy Sirian
9. The Androgynous Andromedan
10. Dancing to the Anunnaki Nookie

Also available in omnibus editions.

UFO Sex Girl

1. The Vegan Virgin
2. The Aphrodisiac Implant *
3. Humping the Hybrid *
4. Licking the Leviathan *
5. Shagging Shiva *
6. Close Encounters of the Reptilian Kind *
7. The Pleaser from the Pleiades *
8. Flying Saucer Love Slave *
9. The Martian Mambo *
10. The Amorous Anunnaki *

*forthcoming

UFO SEX GIRL #1

THE VEGAN VIRGIN

ANN L. PROBE

Horny Alien Press
2014

The Vegan Virgin © 2014 by Ann L. Probe

This edition prepared in 2014 by Horny Alien Press

ISBN-13: 978-1500231934
ISBN-10: 1500231932

Jo Fox walked into the monthly Denver UFO Society meeting as a complete believer. She knew aliens were visiting Earth because her cousin had been performing crazy sex acts with various extraterrestrial beings and telling her about every intimate encounter on their biweekly phone calls. A few months ago, Amy's talks grew shorter and more cryptic, and she sounded more scared than turned on, which was ... well, an alien concept because Amy was a total nympho. Jo was worried. Then the phone calls stopped.

Jo made a few calls to a mutual friend in New York City and found that Amy's apartment had been rented to someone named General Grant T. Gonad, but that friend mentioned that the apartment was empty. Jo knew that meant her friend had used his burglar skills to get inside. Amy left a forwarding address to a post office box, but that box did not exist.

The DUFOS meeting was getting ready to start. Jo paid five bucks to help cover the cost of the room, and took a seat toward the back. The meeting room was in the basement of the Tivoli Student Union of the Auraria campus near downtown, and the people ranged in age from mid-twenties to their eighties. Jo counted sixteen people, mostly white, and noted that a geeky guy at the back was practically undressing her with his eyes. She wondered if the guy had ever seen a woman before. When Jo looked over at him, he blushed and went to fiddling with the keys on his laptop.

A much more attractive man in his early thirties

The Vegan Virgin

stepped up to the podium.

"Hi," the man said. "Welcome to the Denver UFO Society. I'm the director, Barry White—not *that* Barry White obviously." The crowd gave him a polite chuckle, though it was about as amusing as comedian Bill Maher claiming everything was his old job. Barry explained that they had a special guest that afternoon. "Her name is Lissandra Acquarone, and she's here to discuss the Amicizia, or Friendship Case, where human looking extraterrestrials lived and interacted with Italian residents on the shores of the Adriatic Sea. She studied with Professor Stefano Breccia, and we're lucky to have her, so without further ado, please welcome Lissandra."

The people clapped, and Jo joined them, but she kept her eyes on Barry as he took a seat on the other side of the room from her. He met her eyes and gave her a smile and nod, so she looked away.

If Jo didn't already know for sure that aliens were visiting, she might have laughed as Lissandra showed pictures of alleged extraterrestrials, including the semi-famous shot of a man in shorts standing beside a shrub that was supposed to be a tree. Lissandra talked about underground bases near Pescara and how the aliens wanted to be friends and coexisted among the residents of Italy for half a century. Their message was one of hope, friendship, and love. There was nothing that would count as actual evidence, but Jo didn't doubt much of the lecture because Amy had told her about several alien species, some of whom appeared human. She did suspect the love the aliens were talking about was of the physical variety, but she didn't say anything.

The Vegan Virgin

After a Q&A session, the meeting ended, and Jo waited for the crowd to thin a bit before she approached Lissandra.

"Excuse me, Ms. Acquarone," Jo said. "I enjoyed your talk, and I have a few questions."

"Thank you," Lissandra said, meeting her eyes. Jo knew she could have told her she should have asked her questions earlier, but the woman simply smiled. "How can I help you?"

Jo pulled her aside so nobody else could hear. "How would I go about talking to these aliens?"

"Well, they're highly telepathic, and—"

"No, let me rephrase that. How can I meet them?"

"That's the burning question, isn't it? They packed up their base in 1978, so they could be anywhere in the universe by now."

"That doesn't help me."

"I'm sorry," Lissandra said. "We'd all love to meet them. Alas, it's not meant to be."

"My cousin has met them or at least races like them."

Lissandra's eyes went from patience and understanding to *uh-oh, I'm dealing with a Looney Tune* in the space of point five milliseconds. Jo recognized the look, and backed off immediately. After all, if someone talking about aliens secretly living with humans for several decades thinks you're nuts, it's safe to say you're out there in orbit around Pluto without knowing it's no longer even a planet.

"Well," Lissandra said, "it's been nice chatting with you." And she made her escape to the safety of the UFO crowd.

Jo sighed, and turned to leave.

The Vegan Virgin

Barry White stood in the doorway staring at her. "Hello there," he said.

"Um. Hi."

He smiled. "Sorry, I overheard part of your conversation."

Eavesdrop much? Jo thought. "Yeah, about that…"

"You're wondering why someone who talks about non-terrestrial beings living among us would balk at someone else saying a similar thing."

"Well…"

The smile remained on his face. "What's your name?"

"Jo."

"As in Joann?"

"Just Jo. My parents were lazy when they filled out my name on the form."

"Very well, Jo. You accepted what she said, and she clearly didn't accept the same thing from you."

"Yeah. Why is that?"

"It's a question of credibility. She was introduced to the group as someone who studied with a respected professor in the field, but you're just some woman. A mighty attractive woman, but still just a person. And before you accuse me of sexism, you'd have received the same reaction had you been a man."

"If you say so. Still, what she said, with or without the boost from some professor, would have struck me as bullshit six months ago. She wasn't there. She's showing pictures of people claiming they're aliens because that's what she was told. It's all hearsay."

"But you know aliens are among us."

The Vegan Virgin

"Well, yeah."

"How do you know that?"

"Because my cousin knows some of them."

"Has he introduced you to any of them?"

"She. And no."

"Then that, too, is hearsay. Only it comes from someone you trust. If you got to know Ms. Acquarone before you drew the 'let's go meet aliens card,' you could have established some trust and maybe she'd have been inclined to help you."

"I see."

"Of course I say maybe because Ms. Acquarone wouldn't know a non-terrestrial being if she had lunch with one."

"And yet you invited her to speak to your group."

Barry led her outside the room and away from the members of the group still mingling. "We needed a speaker, and she had credentials. Our scheduled guest had to cancel, and I didn't have time to put together a presentation about a famous UFO case, so you play the hand you're dealt."

"Who was your scheduled speaker?"

"Clifford Stone."

"Never heard of him."

"He worked on a crash retrieval team, and—"

"That's something that makes no sense to me," Jo said. "These aliens can fly across the galaxy, but they can't land?"

"Well, the prevailing theory is that when they first arrived, radar messed with their systems."

"Radar? It's radio waves bouncing off an object. The crafts would run into radio waves in space, too, right?"

The Vegan Virgin

"I'm not saying I agree with the theory. Just saying what people tend to believe."

"And what do you believe?"

"I believe I'd like to have dinner with you."

***

Barry took her to Brooklyn's, which was walking distance as it stood practically across the parking lot by the Pepsi Center. They got a booth, ate some good food and had a few drinks. The conversation was the standard getting to know you routine wherein Barry learned that Jo worked as a cashier at a local grocery store, and Jo learned that Barry worked as an engineer in the Tech Center. Both were single. Neither was in a committed relationship. The usual.

"So," Jo said after the waiter took away the empty dishes and brought them each a third drink, "why UFOs?"

"Because I saw one in college," Barry said. "I was out with my frat brothers at a nighttime outdoor party by the lake, and we saw lights in the sky descending toward the water. As the lights grew closer, I could see a craft. It dropped to the center of the lake, then maneuvered around the shoreline, shining its light this way and that, clearly under intelligent control. Then it shot straight up, through the clouds, leaving a hole in them like that craft did at O'Hare a few years back."

"Wait a second. O'Hare as in the Chicago airport?"

"Yes. The O'Hare sighting November 7, 2006. It's arguably the most famous UFO sighting since the Phoenix Lights."

"Why haven't I heard about it?"

The Vegan Virgin

"Maybe you weren't paying attention."

"So it wasn't covered up?"

"The secret of the cover-up is that it's not really covered up. The term cover-up something of a misnomer. You can't cover it up because there are too many witnesses, so instead, the media and most scientists tend to ridicule it. Someone who sees a UFO is considered a crackpot, which means nobody will pay attention to it anymore, and most people don't report them for fear of looking like whackos."

"But aren't most of them a bit on the nutty side?"

"No."

"You think most of them are real?"

"I didn't say that. I think there are hoaxes, but more commonly, I think people misidentify something or simply don't know what something is even when there's a rational explanation like the planet Venus or spotting the International Space Station. At least ninety-five percent of sightings are easily explainable, and that's what we do at DUFOS. We explain away the obvious errors, though we're looking for the five percent that aren't so easily explained."

"Why is it called DUFOS?"

"Because we have a sense of humor about the whole thing, but you don't have to be a doofus to join DUFOS."

"Good because you seem intelligent to me."

"Thank you."

"Do you believe there's a shadow government running the whole UFO show?"

"Like the Bilderbergs?"

"That sounds like the name Amy mentioned."

The Vegan Virgin

"Amy?"

"My cousin. Amy Rush. She..." Jo trailed off because Barry's expression changed. "You've heard of my cousin?"

"Hmm?" Barry said and his face reverted to normal. "No. I can't say as I have."

"I don't believe you."

"Why? Is your cousin famous?"

"No. She's missing."

"What do you mean, missing?" he asked. He looked concerned for a split second.

"She had a job dealing with aliens for the government. She couldn't go into a lot of detail about it, but we were in touch all the time. The last time I heard from her, she sounded scared, or at least concerned for her safety."

"I'm sure she's all right," Barry said.

"How do you know?"

"Because I know how things work, and they don't kill people anymore. It's easier to make them look crazy if they try to be whistleblowers."

"So how do things work?"

"How much do you know about it already?"

"I saw *Close Encounters of the Third Kind* and I watched *The X-Files*. Does that count?"

"I'll give you the Cliff's Notes version, but not tonight."

"Why not tonight? We're here."

He grinned. "Because I really want to see you again, and while I'd love to extend the evening, I have a prior engagement tonight."

"Is that a euphemism for a date?"

"I wish. Sadly, I'm behind on a project at the firm

The Vegan Virgin

and we're going to be working through the weekend to try and complete it by Monday morning. Are you free sometime next week?"

"I want to find my cousin. I came to the meeting today in order to try to find out how to contact the aliens."

"It doesn't work that way."

"There's some doctor on YouTube who said he can contact the aliens."

"And you believe him?"

"Well, he's a doctor."

"That doesn't mean he's not full of shit."

"Can you help me?"

"Jo, if I knew how to contact aliens, I'd have done so many years ago. The UFO group is a sideline thing for me. I've been interested in UFOs since I was a little kid, and when I saw that saucer in college, I was totally hooked. Unfortunately, doing field investigations doesn't pay anything. We're all volunteers. I don't have a TV show and while I have a couple of books out, I don't get paid for speaking engagements. I wish I could help you on that front. I really do."

Jo frowned. "Can you at least point me in the right direction? Is there anyone who actually does know how to contact aliens?"

Barry shook his head. "Anyone who claims to be able to do that is as full of shit as a Thanksgiving turkey. Odds are, the aliens don't pay much attention to humans. We're probably like ants to them."

"That's not what I heard."

"From your cousin?"

Jo nodded.

The Vegan Virgin

"So tell me what you heard."

"No. You'll think I'm crazy."

"You're beautiful enough to get away with being a little crazy. Tell me."

He placed a hand on hers.

She didn't consider herself to be beautiful. She started to pull away, but the soft touch of flesh on flesh felt good, so she changed her mind. "My cousin said the aliens are horny little bastards. Her words, not mine. They're all about getting laid."

"Aren't we all?" he asked, and held her gaze.

She turned away and tugged her hand back.

"Sorry, I didn't mean to offend you," he said.

"You didn't offend me. It's just … well, it's just that nobody's … it's just been awhile. Okay?"

"Hey, I can relate. I haven't even been on a date in three years. I work all the time."

"Your hand must have calluses."

He laughed, and held up his right hand. "I do have to shave my palms."

"I guess I should let you get to work."

"What about this week? I'd still like to see you."

"Are you going to try to get in my pants?"

"You think they'll fit me?"

She rolled her eyes, but she gave him a chuckle, too. He was cute. She could see going to bed with him if the moment was right. "Your project is due Monday, so you'll be wiped out. How does Tuesday sound?"

"It sounds like a date." He gave her a smile.

She found the smile contagious. "It does indeed."

***

Jo didn't make any progress between Saturday and

The Vegan Virgin

Tuesday. She'd agreed to meet Barry at an Olive Garden restaurant in Aurora, and she was pleased that he arrived on time. She was hoping to get lucky tonight, so she'd shaved her legs.

"Italian food after an Italian alien story," he'd said when he chose the location. Jo gave him a quick hug in the lobby.

The dinner was good, though Barry stuck to the salad and breadsticks. Jo really wanted to talk about aliens, and Barry wasn't having any of that. He wanted to know about Jo's life. It felt like standard date conversation, but while she liked him, and did consider this a date, it was also a fact-gathering mission.

After he paid the check, and they exited the restaurant, he gave her a smile. "I have some ideas about how to search for your cousin."

"You do?" she asked.

He nodded. "But we'll need to go to my place to take a look at the books and files that could relate to her missions and possible whereabouts."

"How would you know about her missions?"

"I have contacts in the government. I've written two books about UFO cases and the history of the field, and I've met a lot of people in the know. I mentioned the name Amy Rush to one of my informants, and he said he could help. Do you want to check out the files?"

"I do."

"You want to ride with me or do you want to follow me back to my place?"

"I'll follow you," she said. She wanted to have her car. Barry seemed like a nice enough guy, but she

The Vegan Virgin

wasn't willing to be dependent on him for a ride back. She'd Googled him, of course, so she knew about the books, even though the first search for "Barry White UFO" pulled up a guy named Barry Gray, who did the music for the British television series *UFO*. Jo had never seen the show or listened to the theme music, but wouldn't have been surprised if Barry Gray had been a Gray alien. After all, he also did the theme for *Space 1999*, and both shows had bases on the moon. Many ufologists seemed to believe there was a moonbase. Did the Grays have a base on the moon, too? Maybe it didn't matter.

Barry's house sat on a quiet cul-de-sac in the Village East subdivision of Aurora. It wasn't far from the restaurant. Barry pulled into the garage, but left the door open. Jo parked in the driveway, and climbed out of her car.

Barry exited the garage, looked around a bit, then held out a hand. "Come on in," he said.

She took his hand and let him lead her into the house.

He did not close the garage door.

"Do you want me to catch the door?" she asked, starting to reach for the button.

"No," he said. "The door keeps coming off the track, so I try not to use it much. Since we'll be opening it again before you go, it's best to just leave it up for now."

"Okay," she said. "You might want to get it fixed."

"It's on my to-do list."

He led her to his study, where he had a large file cabinet and a desktop computer with a *Firefly* screen

The Vegan Virgin

saver. He sat in the leather chair before the desk and jiggled the mouse. Nathan Fillion's visage disappeared, replaced by an open Word document. He ignored the document, and clicked on the internet button at the bottom left of his screen. The Google search bar appeared.

"I figure we should start with this," he said and started typing.

Jo looked over his shoulder at the screen. "YouTube?"

"You should get a solid background on the current state of the alien plan."

"You were going to show me something relating to Amy specifically. You were going to help me contact the aliens, or at least put me on the right track. I can watch YouTube videos at home."

"If you could find the right video," he said.

He clicked play, then hit full screen.

The image was dark and grainy. A human male stood in the foreground, looking through a window into a dark room with what looked like a fake alien sitting at an interrogation table.

The title bragged that it was an interview with a real live alien from Area 51. S-4 to be more specific.

"I saw this. It's so lame," Jo said.

"Let it play. This isn't what I wanted you to watch."

"I sure hope not."

"This will need to play for a bit. If I fast forward it, the option will go away."

"Option?"

"I'll show you. But we have some time to kill. Do you want something to drink?"

The Vegan Virgin

"Not really."

"Well, I do. Could you be amazing and get me a bottle of chia water from the refrigerator?"

"All right," she said and went to the kitchen. She opened the refrigerator and saw Vegan butter spread, Fage greek yogurt, extra firm tofu, and a variety of Kombucha drinks and flavored kefir. So Barry was a health food hippie. He'd gone for the salad and breadsticks at the restaurant. Were they gluten free? She didn't know. Did the butter make a difference? All organic or something? Or was he not that strict about it when he was out?

She brought the drink to him.

"Thanks," he said. "Did you get something for yourself, too?"

"I didn't see anything I liked. Are you a vegan?"

His eyes widened for a moment. "I haven't shown you my penis yet, how could you know that?"

"Um. What the fuck?" Jo asked.

"Oh wait, you said vegan, not Vegan. My mistake. Sometimes the pronunciation doesn't register."

Jo started to ease toward the garage door entrance. "I say again, what the fuck?"

"You can't go out that way."

"Yes I can. You left the door open."

"I know, but… Oh! The video is ready, hold on." He hit the alt key and a few others while holding that down and the screen shifted from the bullshit alien interview to what looked like an old video game from the 1980s.

Jo didn't care about the video. She moved toward the door, but when she opened it, she saw three men

The Vegan Virgin

clad in black suits and wearing sunglasses blocking her exit.

"I don't see Will Smith," she said and closed the door in their faces.

"They are Observers."

"What?"

"They like to watch."

"Watch what?"

"Interspecies sex acts. You should really watch this video. It's a man named Nathan Kale who is supposedly an agent with the shadow government, and…"

"Nathan Kale?" Amy had mentioned him so many times. Jo stared at his image on the screen. Yes, she'd open her legs for him.

"You know Agent Kale?"

"No." Then she remembered she wanted to leave. "Tell your Observers to let me pass."

"You want to find your cousin?"

"Of course."

"Then give me a minute."

"I'm not going to watch a video."

He clicked off the monitor. "I don't care. Give me a minute," he said again and began unbuttoning his shirt. "If you still want to go, nobody will stop you."

"What are you doing?" she asked as he removed his shirt and kicked off his shoes.

"Taking off my clothes."

"I can see that."

"So why did you ask?" He unfastened his slacks and let them drop to the floor. He was a boxers man. He tugged them down to reveal a small penis.

The Vegan Virgin

"Oh dear," Jo said. "I realize that we women make jokes about this," she held her fingers apart by two inches, "being ten inches, but dude, that is one tiny little prick."

"It only looks small. Before you take off your clothes and have passionate sex with me in front of the Observers, I need to know how large you like a penis to be before insertion."

"Um. What?"

"My penis is adjustable. I am Barry White from the planet Vega. I apologize, but I have never done this before, so the Observers may need to give me directions. The very sight of you sends amazing sensations to my penis and I would very much like to bring it to full erection before inserting it into your vagina."

"Hold on, Romeo," Jo said. "I'm not going to have sex with you, and if you talk like that, you're going to remain a virgin forever."

"I am a virgin because I saved myself for someone special. You."

"So you're an alien, and not just a twerp with a tiny dick."

"Yes, I lied to you before. Observe." He pulled on his cock and it began to stiffen and grow. He stopped when it stood at full attention and measured a good seven inches. "Is this enough?"

"More," Jo said, though it looked plenty big enough.

"This is actually above the average size for most men."

"More," Jo said again.

He squatted and grabbed his slacks from the floor.

The Vegan Virgin

He pulled a small tube from his pants pocket. He uncapped it and squeezed a gel into his palm. Then he stroked his cock and it began to grow again.

"Won't that make your hand bigger, too?"

"It is designed for my penis, not for my hand. I do not wish to look like a cartoon character."

His cock now stood erect at ten full inches.

"You're an Aerosmith song."

He tilted his head to the side. "The rock and roll band? Dude looks like a lady?"

"Not with that dick," she said. "Big Ten Inch Record." She started to sing the song.

"Would you like to suck on my big ten inch?" he asked.

"This is just weird," Jo said.

"I can make it bigger." He reached for the tube again.

"No. Ten inches is going to hurt."

"Push on the tip. You can adjust the size to whatever you like."

"I don't know. This doesn't even have a smidgen of romance. This would just be fucking."

"You would be doing me a favor. I would be the first Vegan to perform a sex act with a lovely human woman."

"Does that mean Vegans have had sex with human males?"

"Human males will have sex with anything as long as they don't think they'll get caught. Lubricate a knotty tree hole and they will insert a penis."

Jo thought about the men she'd known in her life. In most cases, she suspected the alien was right.

"If you will have sex with me, I will introduce you

The Vegan Virgin

to other aliens and help you find your cousin."

"Do the Observers have to watch?"

"Yes."

"Let me think about it." She stared at his hard cock. "Is that going to go down soon?"

"I can remain hard for as long as you wish."

"I don't know."

"I know for a fact that Amy Rush slept with a ship full of Grays." Jo didn't react, so he added, "The standard aliens known for abducting humans? Big bald heads? Almond shaped eyes? Long spindly arms and legs?"

"The ones who are so into anal?"

"Those are them. I can introduce you to them. We can get a bead on where Amy is by tracking her exploits."

"My ass is exit only."

"Fear not, my aim is true."

"Not you, dipshit. Them."

"Oh." He took a step toward her. "Shall I invite the Observers inside so we can have sex?"

"You're going to have sex with the Observers?"

"I want to have sex with you."

"In front of those Men in Black wannabes?"

"Yes."

Jo shook her head. "Look, you're kinda cute, and I like the whole adjustable penis thing, but I really don't know you, and I'm way too shy to let a bunch of guys watch me have sex."

"But you're beautiful."

"I'm not beautiful," Jo said. "I'm a Plain Jane at best."

"You are beautiful. You are a woman, therefore

The Vegan Virgin

you are beautiful. There is beauty to appreciate in every woman on this planet.'"''

"Oh, you're one of those. You think a mere compliment will get you in my pants."

He stared at her, confused.

"Wait a second," she said. "You're serious."

"Well, yes," he said. "Every woman is beautiful. Some people don't see it, but we do. If I had the time to spend getting to know each woman here, I would fall in love billions of times. Alas, my life is short, and my experience is currently at the zero mark. I am sorry if I offended you. I will get dressed now."

"Wait," Jo said.

He turned to face her.

She hesitated, but finally had to ask, "Do the Observers feel that way, too?"

"The Observers fell in love with humanity. They are not compatible with the inoculations required to make contact with humans. They would die if they touched you, but they like to watch, to bask in the glory of the free spirit during the most intimate times humans can share. They love everyone, but they can't express it beyond watching."

"And you can seriously introduce me to the Grays?"

"Yes, I can contact them."

"So you lied to me before."

"And you lied to me about not knowing anything about aliens. But that is all right. You were trying to protect your cousin who clearly violated her nondisclosure agreement."

"I—"

"We won't tell anyone. We don't care about that.

The Vegan Virgin

We just want to experience the sensual pleasures of the human race. Will you do is this honor?"

Jo took a deep breath. "Invite the Observers in."

"You will perform with me?"

"If you make me feel beautiful."

"I can do that."

The Observers entered the house. Barry led Jo and the guests upstairs to the bedroom. His cock was still hard.

Jo looked at the Observers each in turn and began undressing. She couldn't believe she was doing this. She closed her eyes to avoid their looks as she removed her bra. She kept them closed as she tugged down her panties. When she stood nude before them, she finally opened her eyes and they nodded their approval, but more than that, she could feel them in her mind. They gazed upon her breasts, and while one was bigger than the other, something that had always bothered her, they felt her breasts were gorgeous and perfect for her. They lowered their eyes to her trimmed pubic hair, and their admiration grew. She knew that they knew the time she spent getting it just right, and how much pain went into the waxing in certain areas. While she knew they didn't think she needed to work that hard on something she didn't show many people, they understood that she did it to try to feel good about herself. And the feelings of love they shared in her mind made her feel warm.

She turned around so they could appreciate her ass. She was a little self conscious because she knew she had some cellulite, but they liked that about her, too. She knew their appreciation was genuine, and it made her feel special in a way she'd never felt before.

The Vegan Virgin

Barry approached her. He looked her up and down from head to toe, his eyes resting on her private areas longer than she should have felt comfortable with, but he murmured glowing praise upon her every feature, and finally gazed into her eyes and said with the utmost conviction, "You are an incredibly beautiful woman, Jo. I want to make love with you all night long."

So many men said they wanted to make love to her, not with her. Barry used the word with, and he meant it.

He placed a hand on her bare shoulder and caressed her arm as he moved his fingers toward her hand. His touch was electric, and it left an afterfeeling of cool heat that brought up goosebumps of pleasure. He led her to the bed, and the Observers watched and felt.

Jo didn't feel nervous at all. That was a change because she always felt nervous the first time a man saw her naked. Was she too fat? Was she too skinny? Did she shave well enough? Had she been sweating? Did she wear too much perfume? Oh, the things she could find to worry about were endless, but with Barry, that side of her was silent because with every step and every move, the Observers and Barry himself sent her waves of love and appreciation.

Barry pulled her close and tasted her lips. She returned the kiss, and felt the give of his flesh. She felt his hardness against her and she reached for it, molded it to the size she wanted—something that would fit her well, but not hurt so much to avoid the pleasure. He was content to kiss her all over, but she needed him inside her. She'd never felt such a strong

The Vegan Virgin

need.

She stretched out before him and he moved atop her. She kept hold of his cock and guided him inside. As he slid into her, the feeling was like a tsunami crashing through her. She felt elation and delight and desire and a pleasure beyond what she could describe. He moved in and out in a steady rhythm, and each thrust was like a wave crashing on her beach of loneliness. In came the good feelings, and out went the bad. He pushed in and pulled out and she moved with him, undulating and crying out and actually crying. She felt the tears roll down her cheeks. Tears of joy. Barry kissed them away, tasted the saltiness and shared the flavor with her as his own tears leaked from his eyes.

"You are the most amazing woman I've ever known," he whispered. "You are loveliness embodied."

While he wasn't much of a poet, his sincerity made up the difference, and the Observers tripled the feelings. She chanced a glance at them as Barry nibbled on her right nipple. The Observers worked their mouths as if they too were tasting her. She glanced down to make sure they weren't beating off. Then again, if they had been, she wasn't sure she'd have minded because she could feel their thoughts and she knew they found her to be as beautiful as Barry said.

Sweat beaded on her body and pooled between her breasts, and Barry licked it up and smiled at her and she felt loved. He rolled over so she was on top, and she writhed back and forth, taking him as deep as she wanted. She found herself wishing he could grow

The Vegan Virgin

just a little bit larger. His cock grew inside her.

"Your wish is my command," he whispered.

And she began wishing, and every wish was fulfilled in that bed. He was gentle and rough and fun and serious at the exact moments she needed him to be. He felt her emotions and she felt his. He loved everything about her, and she loved him right back.

They laughed, they cried.

His cock was like a magic wand and his lips were like soft incantations of spells, and oh dear God his tongue. Oh, when he moved down her body, kissing her lightly, caressing her flesh, moving his tongue down her landing strip to the moist and juicy entrance to her love, she felt sensations that shot her like a rocket into space, and when his tongue moved in elegant circles around her clit, she lost sight of the room, forgot about the Observers, and felt like she was being handled by the tongue of a god.

She cried out.

He kept circling.

She squirmed, but didn't have to guide him, and at the precise moment she was ready, his tongue pressed into her button and she erupted like Mount Vesuvius.

"Goodbye, Pompeii," she whispered when she could find her voice again.

She lay in a puddle of her own love juice. Barry gently moved her to a dry spot, and began stroking her body with tender caresses that made her feel safe and kept her floating. A moment later, she realized she actually was floating a few inches above the bed.

"You have made my first time the best imaginable," Barry whispered. "And I will always love you."

The Vegan Virgin

She felt the moments stretch as he held her and caressed her and felt the Observers basking in her glory at the same time.

They all loved her completely in those moments. They loved her look, her smell, her taste, her sounds.

A little later, when she was feeling more like herself, she asked, "Did you come?"

"I came in ways you could not understand." He hesitated. "Or perhaps you can." And he opened his mind a bit so she could feel what he had felt as they made love. He felt accepted, and he felt her appreciation for the way he made her feel, and that gave him what she perceived as an ejaculation of the soul that could tide him over for eternity. "To give pleasure is to receive pleasure," he said.

And for him she knew it was true.

The Observers, knelt before her and bowed their heads. They send her a telepathic thank you that filled her soul and she knew that for as long as she lived she would never worry about how she looked to anyone else because to them she was perfect. And that was enough.

***

The next morning, Jo awoke in Barry's arms. He was already awake, and perhaps had never even slept. He simply held her and gazed into her eyes with love and admiration.

"I will help you find your cousin," he said.

"Thank you."

"The journey will not be easy, and you must be aware that most of the alien races we encounter will require sexual favors in order to help us in our quest. Are you okay with that?"

The Vegan Virgin

"I feel fine with it right now, but I don't know how I'll feel when the time arrives. Will I always feel this good or is this moment as fleeting as all moments?"

"Feelings fade to pleasant memories, but I will be with you to recreate the feelings," Barry said. "I will share you with the galaxy if you are willing, and I will keep you safe and I will love you for all eternity. I am not jealous, and I do not require your love in return. You are free to do as you please when you please, but if you want my help, you will need to accept my guidance."

"I trust you," she said. And she felt that trust was well-placed because she knew he loved her and would never allow her to come to any permanent harm. "I do have one request."

"Name it," he said.

"If any of these beings make me feel bad, will you make love with me to take that away again?"

"You're the first, my last, my everything," he said.

She smiled. "The Observers are gone."

"Yes, they went back to the Mothership."

"In that case, let's make love again. This time for only us."

She kissed him and reached for his adjustable cock.

He smiled.

**The UFO Sex Girl series continues with
The Aphrodisiac Implant**

Ann L. Probe is the author of The Alien Sex Chronicles series and is currently working on the followup, UFO Sex Girl, another set of ten alien erotica stories. Ann lives on a flying saucer where she satisfies her desires by sleeping with aliens herself. Field research is such a joy! Visit her online at annlprobe.com and sign up for her newsletter to get a free ebook edition of *How to Get Abducted by UFO Aliens: A Short and Stubby Guide to Having Sex with Extraterrestrials.* Wow, the title is almost as long as the ebook!

Made in the USA
Las Vegas, NV
26 July 2022